STORYBOTS®

WHY DO WE RECYCLE?

Written by Scott Emmons
Designed by Mark Warnick

A Random House PICTUREBACK® Book

Random House 🏠 New York

© 2022 Netflix, Inc. All rights reserved. Published in the United States by Random House Children's Books, a division of Penguin Random House LLC, 1745 Broadway, New York, NY 10019, and in Canada by Penguin Random House Canada Limited, Toronto.
Pictureback, Random House, and the Random House colophon are registered trademarks of Penguin Random House LLC. StoryBots, Netflix, and all related titles, logos, and characters are trademarks of Netflix, Inc.
rhcbooks.com
ISBN 978-0-593-48337-4 (trade) — ISBN 978-0-593-48338-1 (ebook)
Printed in the United States of America
10 9 8 7 6 5 4 3 2 1

Hap was at his workstation, barking answers into multiple phones. "Banana! Bandanna! Gary, Indiana!" But then he got a tricky question. "What? . . . Send me the best answer team we've got!"

Bing, Bang, Beep, Bo, and Boop dropped from the transport tube.

"Don't just stand there!" cried Hap. "We just got a doozy of a question! 'Why do people have to recycle?'"

"Boop! Boop!" said Boop, rushing to the keypad and punching in a series of numbers.

"Outerworld, here we come!" the StoryBots shouted. The tube drew them in . . .

. . . and dumped them into a bin full of garbage. Filthy, rotting, stinking garbage!

"Why did you bring us here, Boop?" asked Bang. But Boop couldn't answer. He had a yogurt container stuck on his head.

Soon they were loaded onto a garbage truck, which dumped them on the biggest, grossest, stinkiest pile of trash they had ever seen!

To make things worse, a bulldozer
was speeding toward them!

Just then, a car skidded to a stop in front of them.
"Get in!" said the giant cockroach who was driving.
The StoryBots jumped in, and they all sped away.

"They call me Angry Annie," said the driver when they were safe. "Angry because I live in a dirty, stinking landfill."
"What's a landfill?" asked Beep.
"It's where humans dump their trash," Annie grumbled.

"Boop!" said Boop. He had finally freed himself from the container. It left a strange mark with three arrows on his head.

"I know that symbol!" cried Annie. "He's the one we've been waiting for! I must take him to Lord Wormo!"

Lord Wormo led a scrappy band of rats and other animals who lived among the garbage. "Greetings, StoryBots," he said. "This land was once called the Green Place. Then came the humans with their garbage, turning it into this wasteland.

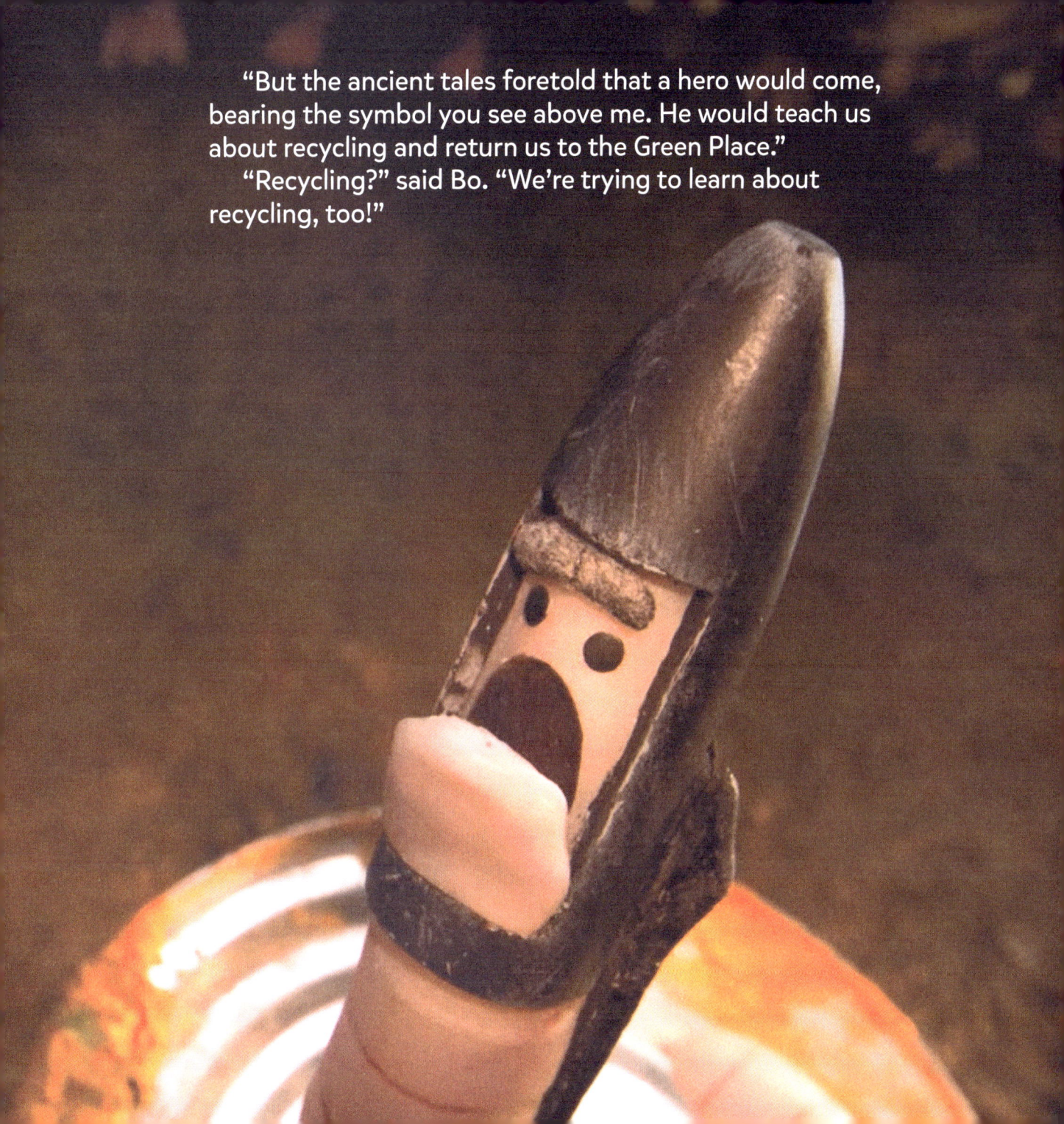

"But the ancient tales foretold that a hero would come, bearing the symbol you see above me. He would teach us about recycling and return us to the Green Place."

"Recycling?" said Bo. "We're trying to learn about recycling, too!"

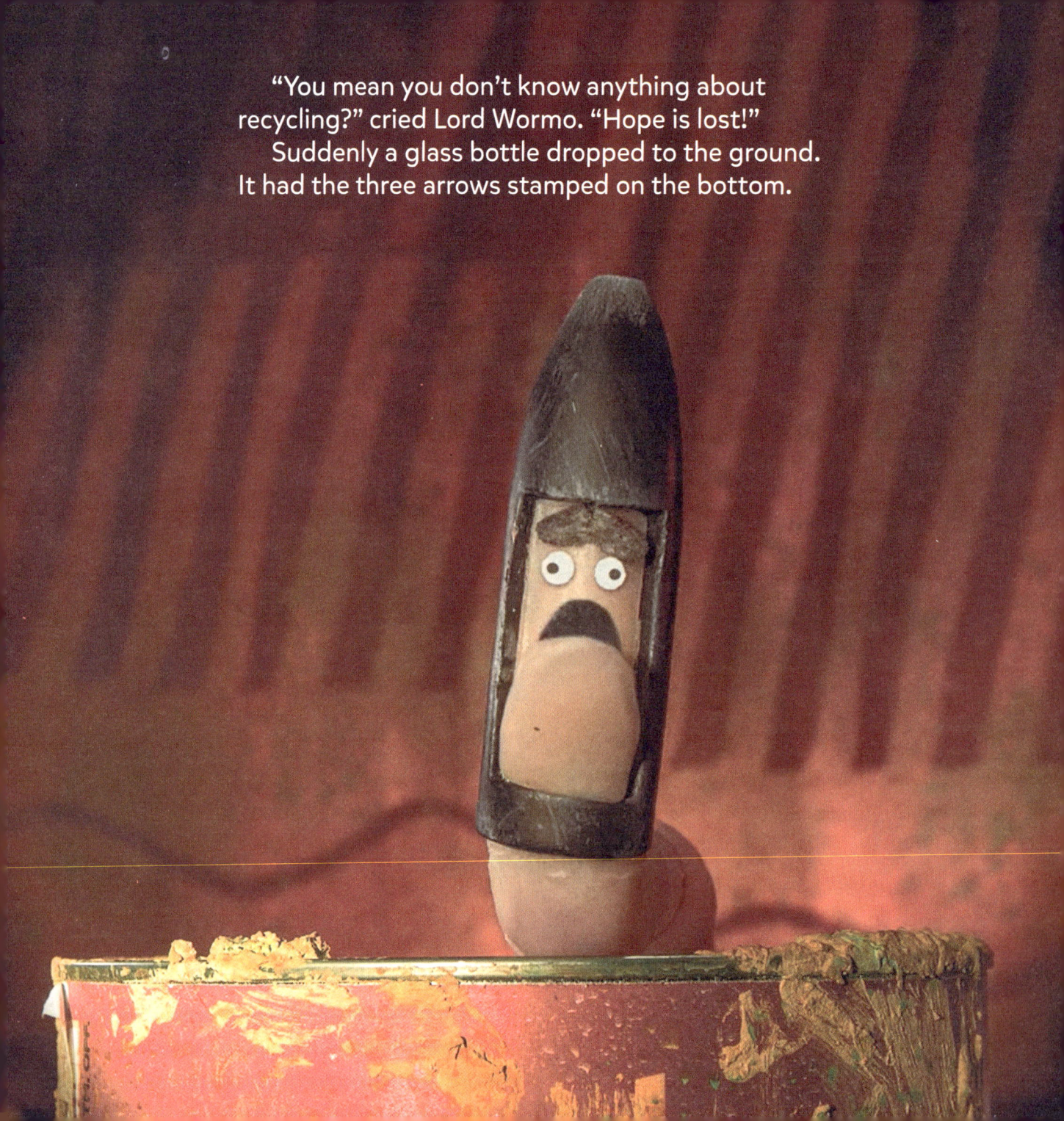

"You mean you don't know anything about recycling?" cried Lord Wormo. "Hope is lost!"
Suddenly a glass bottle dropped to the ground. It had the three arrows stamped on the bottom.

When the StoryBots looked through it,
they saw the same symbol in the distance.

"Let's check it out!" said Beep.
Annie drove up in her car.
"Let's ride!" she said.

They raced over heaps of trash. Annie drove straight up the scoop of a bulldozer, and then they were flying. From high above the landfill, they could see a beautiful, brightly colored building with the symbol at the top.

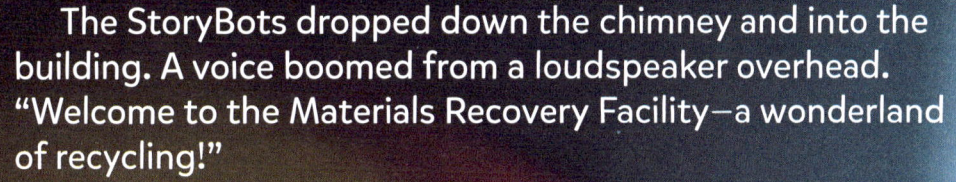

The StoryBots dropped down the chimney and into the building. A voice boomed from a loudspeaker overhead. "Welcome to the Materials Recovery Facility—a wonderland of recycling!"

"Recycling?" said Beep. "That's what we're trying to learn about!"

"Come in," said the voice, "and you'll learn all about it!"

"First, giant spinning rollers keep the lighter materials—like cardboard and paper—bouncing along the top. Heavier materials—like metal, plastic, and glass—fall below!

"All those heavier items pass an enormous spinning magnet. It snags metals like steel, tin, and iron.

"Next, an optical scanner separates plastic from glass. It finds the plastic items and uses blasts of air to carry them away.

"The glass, which is heavier, falls below again.

"Now that the materials are separated, they are ready to be shipped to factories, where they'll be made into new stuff. That's what recycling is!"

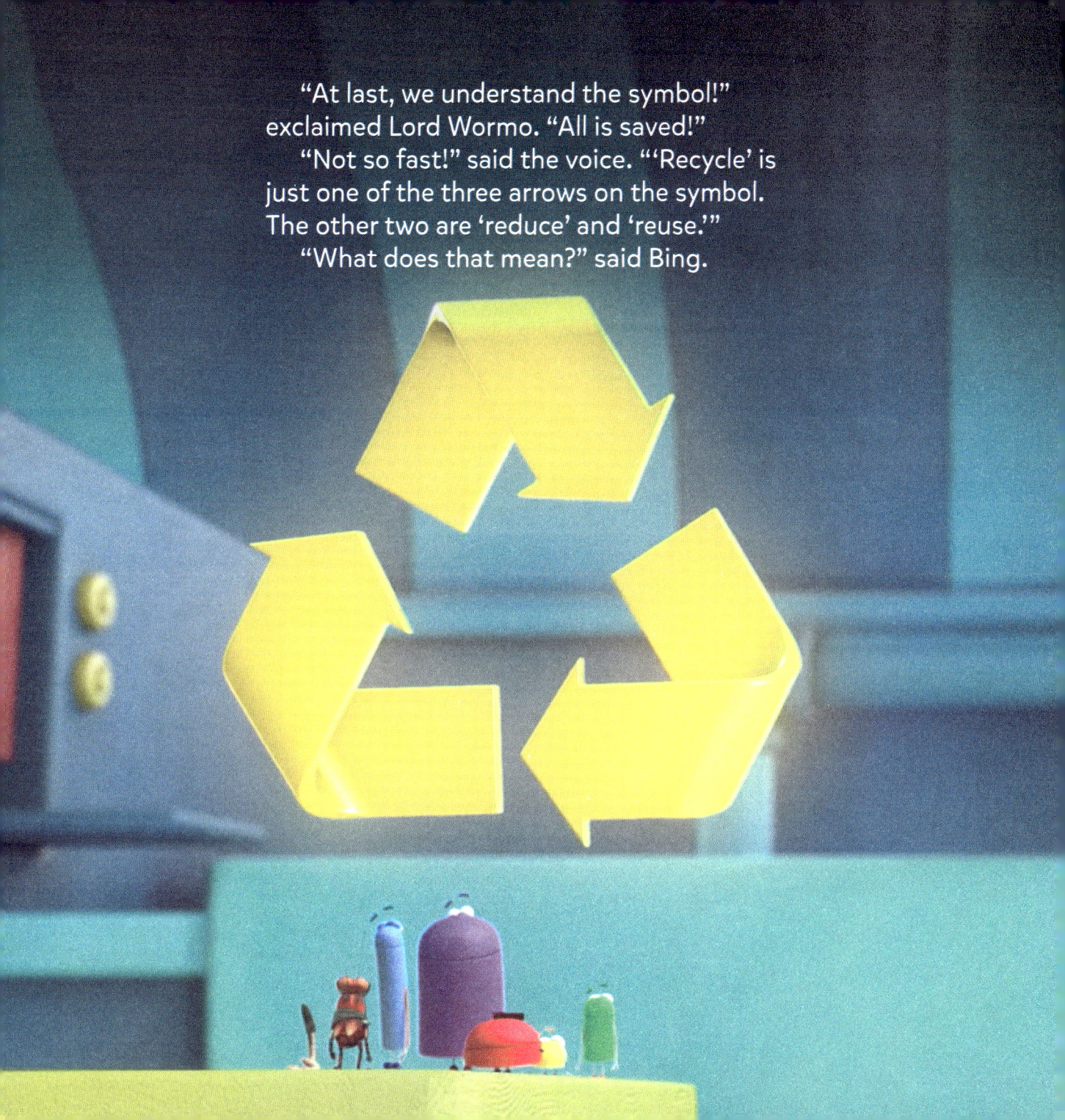

"At last, we understand the symbol!" exclaimed Lord Wormo. "All is saved!"

"Not so fast!" said the voice. "'Recycle' is just one of the three arrows on the symbol. The other two are 'reduce' and 'reuse.'"

"What does that mean?" said Bing.

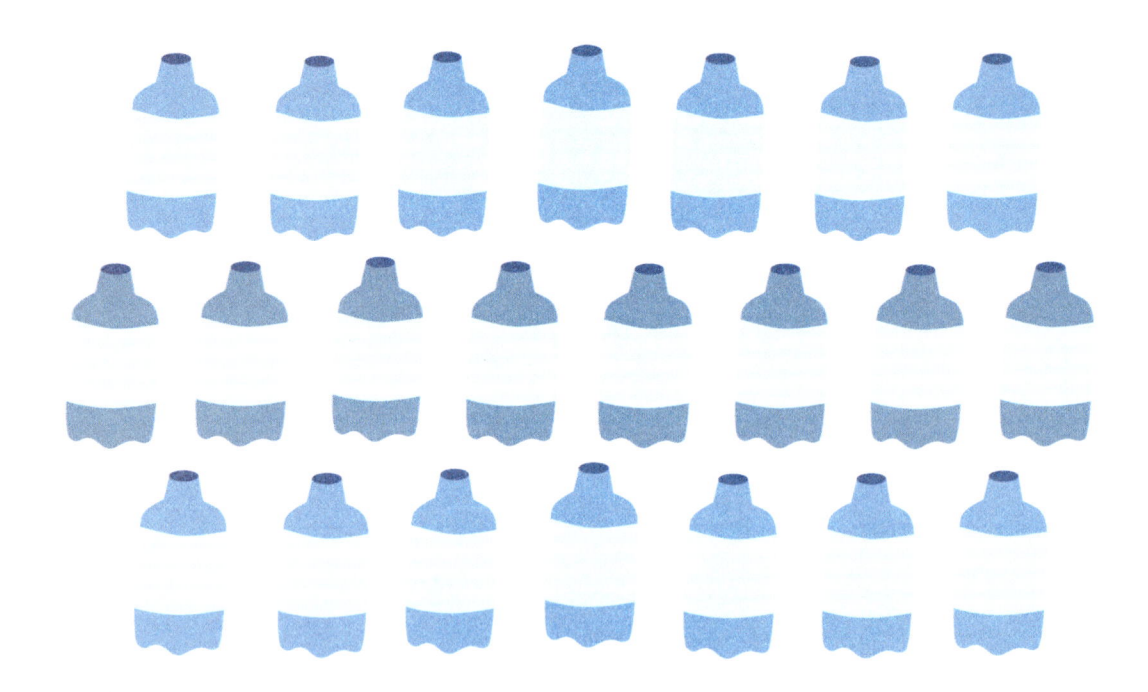

"First," said the voice, "you need to 'reduce' the amount of trash you create. Instead of using lots of plastic bottles, you can use one glass!"

"That would put a lot less trash into the landfill!" said Beep.

"What about 'reuse'?" asked Bang.

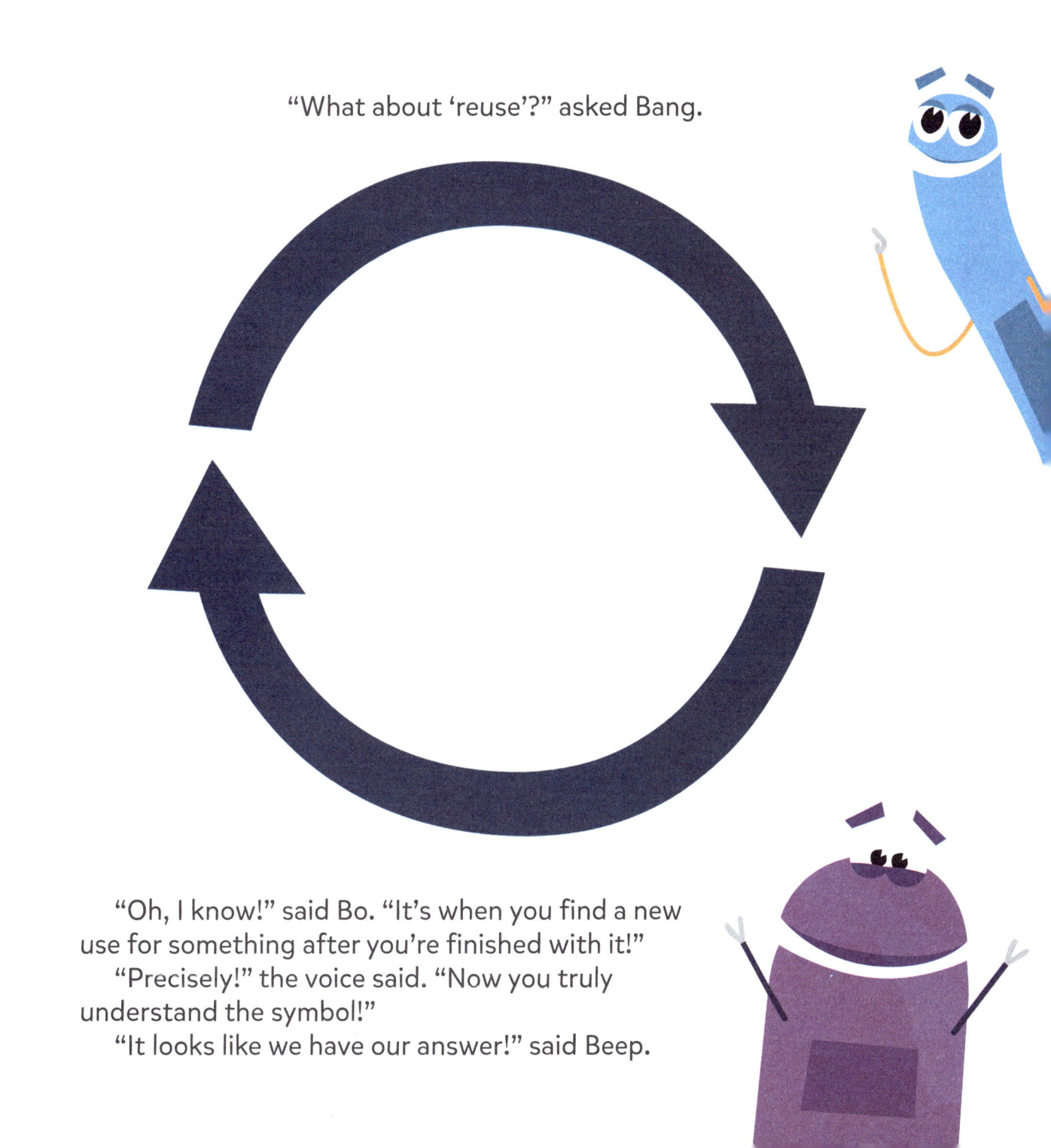

"Oh, I know!" said Bo. "It's when you find a new use for something after you're finished with it!"

"Precisely!" the voice said. "Now you truly understand the symbol!"

"It looks like we have our answer!" said Beep.

Hap was surprised to see the team return so quickly. "What are you doing back here?" he growled.

"We got the answer, Boss," said Beep. "We know why people need to recycle!"

"And reduce and reuse," added Bang.

Hap sighed impatiently. "Just give me the tape."

Hap watched the video and saw how trash in a landfill damages the environment. He learned that people could *reduce* the amount of trash they threw away, *reuse* items, and *recycle* materials to make new stuff. "Reduce, reuse, and recycle," he said. "I think I just learned something!"

"Mission accomplished," said Beep. "Great job, team!"
"Enough jibber-jabber, StoryBots!" cried Hap. "We've got questions to answer! Move! Now! Go! Work! Move!"

"Whoa," said Bang. "He should, like, *reduce* his stress level!"